A Lion for a Sitter

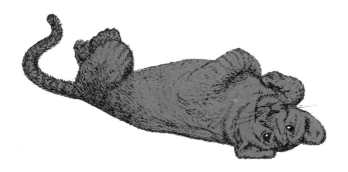

by Helen Kay
pictures by Yaroslava

ABELARD-SCHUMAN

LONDON   NEW YORK   TORONTO

For Michelle, Erin and Andrew

"Who is going to sit with me?" asked Andrew.

"Try and guess," said Mother.

Andrew, bathed and washed and tucked into bed,
tried to think.

"I'll give you a hint," said Mother.

"It's the very best sitter in the whole wide world."

Andrew heard the sound of Father's old car
going for the sitter,

clangety, bangety.

Who would he bring back?

"Is it...is it...is it a LION?" asked Andrew.

"He'd be cozy and warm."

"Oh, no," Mother said,
"but if you were a lion cub,
you'd be their pride.
They'd find a lion to sit for you.
Lions are very good sitters for lion cubs."

Andrew tried again.

"Is it a dolphin?" asked Andrew.
"We could swim all the time."

"Oh, no," Mother said,
"but if you were a baby dolphin,
you'd swim in between your mother and
another dolphin. They would take care of you."

Andrew knew he wasn't a dolphin.
Besides, he couldn't swim very well.

"Is it an ostrich?" asked Andrew.
(He was remembering all the animals he had
seen at the zoo.)

"Oh, no," Mother said,
"but if you were an ostrich chick,
an ostrich father would watch over you.
He would not care which mother hen had
hatched you."

Andrew snarled and bared his teeth.
"Is it a gorilla, GRRR..?" he asked.

Now he was afraid. He hid under the bed.
He was sure Mother would have to say, "No."

"Oh, no," Mother said,
"but if you were a little gorilla,
your mother would hold you close until
you could cling. Then she would carry you
piggyback wherever she went. If she were
not there, another gorilla would let you
share a ride on her back."

"Just one more guess," said Mother.
She heard their old car coming back,

bangety, clangety.

"Is it a giraffe?" asked Andrew, and he
laughed at the thought. How could a giraffe
get into their little house?

"Oh, no," Mother said,
"but if you were their calf, other giraffes
would look out over the trees
to see what was coming from far away."

Now Andrew heard Father's footsteps on
the stairs. But who was stamping behind him,

thump, thump,

thump and bump?

Suddenly, Andrew knew.

"Don't open the door!" he cried.

"It's an elephant!"

Father opened the door, just a crack....

"Oh, no," Father said,
"but if you were a baby elephant,
your elephant aunt might sit for you,
or another elephant who might be
your grandmother."

"How would you like me for a sitter?" asked
a very loud voice. And Andrew's real
grandmother came into the room.
Andrew liked it very much.

He did not care when Father and Mother
softly closed the door and went away.

"But, Grandmother," Andrew asked,
"what was that thumping up the stairs
behind you?"
Grandmother's eyes twinkled as she said,
"I could not find a sitter for Lion.
He's lonely when I leave him at home."

Then she went to the door
and called, "Lion!"

And a big shaggy dog jumped up on the bed,
knocked Andrew down on the pillow and
licked his face.

SHHHH......